VELDA THE AWESOMEST VIKING

To my Viking pals in P4 at Raploch Primary,
Stirling, and Mrs Hann – D.M.

For Harriet and all the Little Vikings
in Viking House! – R.M.

Kelpies is an imprint of Floris Books
First published in 2021 by Floris Books

Text © 2021 David MacPhail. Illustrations © 2021 Floris Books
David MacPhail and Richard Morgan have asserted their rights under the
Copyright, Designs and Patent Act 1988 to be identified as the Author and
Illustrator of this Work. All rights reserved. No part of this book may be
reproduced without the prior permission of Floris Books, Edinburgh
www.florisbooks.co.uk

 Also available as an eBook

British Library CIP Data available
ISBN 978-178250-717-8
Printed and bound by MBM Print SCS Ltd Glasgow

 Floris Books supports sustainable forest management
by printing this book on materials made from wood that
comes from responsible sources and reclaimed material

MIX
Paper from
responsible sources
FSC® C117931
www.fsc.org

VELDA THE AWESOMEST VIKING

and the Voyage of DEADLY Doom

Written by **David MacPhail**

Illustrated by **Richard Morgan**

Young Kelpies

Straits of Incredible DANGER
NORWAY
Island of Certain Death
Port Hengist
GAUL
BRITAIN

Chapter 1

It was the Dark Ages, when kings and queens went stumbling around their pitch-black castles shouting, "Help! Where am I? Who turned out the lights?"

The Vikings spread terror across the seas thanks to their fearsome dragonships and their even more fearsome **BELCHING**.

The most feared of all the Viking dragonships was the *Valkyrie* – a sleek, sturdy vessel with a sail of red-and-white stripes. The *Valkyrie* was crewed only by women, whose belching was so terrifying it could frighten mermen half to death.

The captain was a tall, blonde-haired woman called Freya. She was the noisiest and stinkiest belcher of all. Like most captains, she liked to gaze out to sea a lot with her hands on her hips, giving loud, hearty laughs, as you would if you were living a life of adventure and scaring people silly.

One day, as the *Valkyrie* was sailing the great Northern Sea, Freya turned to her helmswoman, Brunhilda of Barfhelm, and said, "Set sail for the Island of Certain Death!"

"OORAH!" cried her crew.

"OORAH!" echoed the youngest and newest crew member, Velda of Indgar. The tiny girl with thick red hair poking out from under a too-big helmet pumped her fist with glee. "YES! Certain death, *finally*!"

Velda rummaged around in her pack before festooning herself with leafy camouflage (for sneaking purposes), coils of rope and a grappling hook (for climbing-somewhere-you-probably-weren't-meant-to-be purposes), and last but most definitely not least, weapons (for terrifying-people-until-they-cried purposes).

She leapt in front of Freya, whirling a gigantic axe around her head. "I am SOOOOOO ready for certain death, Boss!"

Freya gave another of her hearty laughs. "You don't have to worry, Velda."

Velda sliced the air with her axe. "Worry?! Are you kidding? This is exactly why I joined your crew. This is my chance to be a *real* Viking."

"You *are* a real Viking," said Freya. "That's why I took you aboard."

"Yeah, but girls were never allowed to do any of the fun Viking-y stuff back home in Indgar. It was always 'Don't yell so much, Velda!', 'Practise your weaving, Velda!', 'Stop trying to kill people you don't like, Velda!' Then they tried to confiscate my axe. That was the last straw." And it really was, for Velda had chopped the wheel off the village hay wagon in a fit of anger, sending Indgar's entire winter supply tumbling into the fjord. Velda didn't run from *anyone*, but she'd just happened to decide on a life at sea at the exact moment she'd been chased by angry villagers with torches and pitchforks.

Freya sat Velda down on a bench, placing a hand on her shoulder. "You know, some things aren't always what they seem."

"What does that mean?"

"You'll see," smiled Freya. "We're not your average Viking crew here on the *Valkyrie*."

They really weren't. Their legendary feats were spoken of far and wide: how they'd battled the Kraken of Corrievreckan, taken on the Terrible Trolls of Tromsø, and even stolen into the great hall of the Dwarf-Lords and nicked their famous golden underpants.

Velda reckoned the Island of Certain Death would be a picnic for this crew – and she was itching to prove she was Viking enough to be one of them.

Chapter 2

The Island of Certain Death soon came into sight, but it wasn't quite what Velda had been expecting. There were no doom-laden skies, no ominous cracks of lightning, not even a mangy fire-breathing dragon or two. The Island of Certain Death was instead perfectly picturesque, with lush green trees edging a sandy white beach and a neat pier. At the head of the pier stood a gateway to a wooden fort.

"You stay here, Velda," said Freya as she strode off up the gangplank. "Guard the ship and look after our old and sick."

"WHAT?! Why me?!" Velda protested. "I've been practising my double-swoop-underarm-axe throw specially!"

But no matter how much she wanted to, Velda couldn't disobey an order from her captain. Instead, she had to watch as Freya and the rest of the crew paraded off the boat, smiling and laughing (and belching, obviously). She couldn't help but notice that they weren't very well armed for facing certain death.

They carried no swords or spears, just small cloth bundles tucked under their arms.

"AAAARGGH!" Velda screamed with rage, then swung her axe and sunk it into one of the colourful shields that lined the side of the longship.

THWOCK!

"Something ails you?" asked Henna of Greenland. The *Valkyrie*'s oldest crew member, Henna had been a legendary fighter in her day, and still carried her

long, curved Inuit bow. Now the only thing she was legendary for was her cabbagey farts.

"It's not *fair*!" growled Velda.

"I once got trapped on a deserted island with only a reindeer for company," Henna said, staring out to sea. "I had to drink its wee. That also wasn't fair."

"What did the reindeer drink?" asked Velda, curious.

"My wee," replied the old woman.

"You know what else isn't fair?" chirped Nissa of Coldfjord, the only other crew member left behind. Nissa's Viking helmet perched on top of a thick wad of bandages. Velda had heard a story from the crew that she'd been nibbled by a polar bear, but thought they might have been joking with her.

"What?" Velda snapped.

Nissa opened her mouth to speak, but then a confused look came over her face. "Oh, er… I've forgotten." She scratched her bandaged head. "Sorry, sometimes it happens when I'm in the middle of a… a… a…"

"Sentence?"

"Hmm?" Nissa's attention wandered. "Ooh, look! Doesn't that cloud look like an enormous bottom?"

Before Velda could throw herself overboard in frustration, the sound of a blood-curdling scream echoed from inside the fort.

"AAAAIIIIEEEE!"

"Great Thor! The crew's in danger!" cried Velda. Without the slightest hesitation, she straightened her helmet, pulled her axe from the splintered shield, and leapt over the side of the ship.

Chapter 3

Velda sprinted up the pier, looking rather like a murderous garden shrub. She unslung her grappling hook and began to twirl it around her head. She was aiming for the fort's battlements, but then she spied the main gate lying ajar…

"A-HA!" She somersaulted through the gap and expertly landed in a squat, axe raised.

"HEY!" cried a man in a red tunic, probably one of the guards. His poor gatekeeping would cost him. Velda leapt in the air, then knocked him to the ground with a high kick.

"HI-YAAA!"

Another man in red charged towards her, waving his arms and shouting, "STOP!" This time she dived low, sweeping him off his feet. The man screamed in panic. "A bush! I'm being attacked by a bush!"

A third man came at her, wielding what appeared to be a giant sausage. He looked confused, and that made two of them, for Velda had never fought a man armed with a sausage before. She clubbed him with the blunt end of her axe and he crashed against a wooden hut, scattering objects across the ground.

There was suddenly chaos everywhere, with people running and screaming. Then the crowd slowly parted and standing in front of Velda was Freya. Her hair was tied up in a bun and she was wearing a swimming tunic and a pair of fish-flops

on her feet. She did not look pleased.

"Velda, what are you doing?!"

Velda took a moment to survey the scene. Only now did she glimpse a turquoise lake behind Freya's shoulder, some of the *Valkyrie*'s crew lounging at its edge, sipping from drinking horns with little umbrellas poking out of the top. Other crew members

splashed around in the water, taking turns on a rope swing. It slowly dawned on Velda – *that's* where the screams were coming from! They weren't screams of pain, they were screams of excitement: the joyful cries of people doing somersaults and belly flops.

Velda stared at the carnage behind her. The two men she'd thought were armed guards were just doorkeepers. The man with the sausage was – duh! – an elk-hot-dog-salesman. The hut he'd fallen against was a gift shop, and the objects scattered on the ground were souvenirs – novelty silver drinking horns, furry helmet warmers, even shirts with funny slogans embroidered across the front, like: 'I SURVIVED CERTAIN DEATH AND ALL I GOT WAS THIS LOUSY TUNIC'.

It was some kind of Viking holiday resort!

"Certain death, my eye!" growled Velda, swiping

her axe and angrily chopping the head off a Viking-helmet-wearing souvenir garden gnome.

Back on the ship, Freya sat with a despondent Velda. Velda had removed the leafy camouflage, though she kept her axe close, just in case a tiny bit of certain death was lurking around somewhere.

"Didn't I tell you things aren't always as they seem?" said Freya. "If you scratch under the surface, you often find something quite different beneath. It's called the Island of Certain Death for a reason – to scare non-Viking folk away. It's where we go to relax. It's hard work having a fearsome reputation."

"Does this mean I'm not going to be doing any fighting?" asked Velda sadly.

Freya laughed. "Oh, don't worry, there's plenty of that. But there's more to being a Viking than battles and belching." She squeezed Velda's arm then yelled over at her second-in-command, Sigrid of Sneezegaard. "Set sail for the Straits of Incredible Danger!"

"OORAH!" cried the crew.

Velda's face lit up. "Did you say 'Straits of Incredible Danger'?!" It wasn't nearly as good as certain death, but it would do.

Freya scrunched her nose and tilted her head from side to side. "Mmm, I wouldn't get your hopes up too much…"

Velda sighed. Would she ever get the chance to be a *real* Viking?

Chapter 4

The *Valkyrie* began its passage through the narrow Straits of Incredible Danger towards the open sea. Velda glared sullenly from the prow as two great headlands rose up on either side, seabirds swirling around the cliffs. As expected, there wasn't a sniff of danger about the place, not even a bit of mild peril, which was *so* depressing! She ripped off her helmet in frustration. "Uhh!"

"You know what I think?" It was Nissa again. "I think you're in a… a… a… OH!" Her face lit up as they left the straits and the sea opened out before them. "What lovely scenery…"

"A bad mood!" snapped Velda. "I'm in a VERY. BAD. MOOD!"

"I once met a chicken that was in a bad mood," said Henna, who was oiling her bow nearby.

"How could you tell it was in a bad mood?" asked Velda.

"Because I shot it with an arrow," she replied with a shrug.

They all stared in silence at the horizon.

A shadow suddenly crossed the deck, blotting out the sun. There was a huge **CRASH!** and the boat shuddered, throwing them off their feet. Velda looked up, amidst a shower of sea spray and splintered wood, to see the prow of a giant ship looming over them. A prow in the shape of a ram's head.

A ram's head? thought Velda. *Viking ships have ferocious dragons on their prows, not mangy sheep…*

"Saxons!" shouted Nissa matter-of-factly over the din.

"Huh?"

"Saxons have ram's heads on their prows." Nissa screwed up her face. "Wait... How did I know that?"

Another **CRASH!** and a second vessel smashed into the other side of the boat. The *Valkyrie* was pinned between two enormous warships.

"We've been ambushed!" cried Freya.

"They must have come round the headland to launch a surprise attack," added Nissa, before her face screwed up a second time. "Wait – how did I know that, too?"

"I was once attacked by surprise," said Henna in her deep voice. "By a ferret. I do not like surprises." She stroked a suspiciously ferrety-looking fur hanging around her shoulders.

Soldiers leapt off the Saxon vessels and onto the *Valkryie*, their swords flailing. A battle cry went up, and Freya's crew snatched their weapons and flew into the fight. But they were surrounded and outnumbered.

Not that it bothered Velda. Her bad mood had totally disappeared; she hadn't been this excited in weeks! "Finally, a battle!" she cried, cracking her knuckles and grabbing her axe. She was just about

to launch a perfect roundhouse kick on a terrified Saxon soldier when Freya rushed over and picked her up, bundling her away to the ship's stern.

"NOOO! Wrong way! You're taking me the WRONG WAY!" yelled Velda, swishing her axe through the air.

"Not for you!" Freya righted her and stuffed a folded-up piece of parchment under Velda's helmet.

"I need you to take this!"

"What is it?" Velda asked sulkily.

"You'll figure it out." Freya hurriedly pressed a money pouch into Velda's hand and then pushed her over the side of the ship. "Now go!"

"BUT—" Velda protested, clinging onto the edge.

"No buts! That's an order!" Freya turned to Nissa and Henna. "You two, go with her."

Freya rushed back into the battle, while Nissa obediently climbed over the *Valkyrie*'s side. Henna followed after her.

As they dangled above the waves, a woman's voice rose over the chaos, an ear-piercing, operatic screech that went *high* then *low* then *high* again, before hovering like an annoying wasp. It cut through the sounds of clashing swords to bring the fighting to a complete standstill.

Everyone stopped, mid-fight, to jam their fingers in their ears and look up. Perched on top of a Saxon prow was a woman with the longest hair Velda had ever seen. She wore expensive-looking robes and a breastplate so shiny it startled a flock of seabirds overhead. On her head rested a glittering golden crown.

"YOU!" she bellowed, pointing an accusing finger at Freya. "Where is my Silver Tusk?"

Chapter 5

"We made a deal!" the woman bellowed at Freya. "All you had to do was find me that teensy little Silver Tusk. In return, I'd give you as much gold as your grubby Viking hands could carry. Was that too much to ask?"

Freya glared defiantly at the lady. "I gave you my word. But you need to give me more time—"

"Your word? PAH!" the woman replied. "I'm fed up of waiting!"

"I'm sorry, but you'll just have to wait a little longer," said Freya with a shrug.

The lady's eyes bulged and her cheeks reddened, then she let loose a ginormous high-pitched scream,

"AAAARGGHHIEEEE!", shattering the glass in the small lantern that hung off the Valkyrie's mast with a **SMASH**!

"Who is *she*?" whispered Velda, still hanging over the *Valkyrie*'s side with Nissa and Henna. "She's got a voice like a strangled albatross!"

"Ethelfled, Queen of Kent," said Nissa, before she gave a little start. "Oh, how did I know that?"

The Saxon queen's nostrils flared. "I knew I should never have trusted a sly, stinking Viking. Well, I hope you like rats, because it's the castle dungeons for you and your crew!"

"Who's she calling stinking?!" Velda's face turned crimson. "Queen or no queen, she's getting it!" She rolled up her sleeves and began to vault over the side, but Henna stopped her.

"Wait, wasn't there something we were supposed to look after?" asked Nissa absent-mindedly.

Velda suddenly remembered the parchment Freya had stuffed under her helmet. Grrr, she wanted nothing more than to teach this shrieking Saxon a royal lesson, but Freya had given her an order…

"UGH. Fine!" Velda harrumphed. "Let's go." She **PLOPPED** into the freezing water alongside Nissa and Henna, watching as Ethelfled's ships sailed off towards the horizon, dragging the *Valkyrie* and her imprisoned crew behind them.

Chapter 6

After a long, cold swim, the three fugitives finally washed up on the craggy shore. Nissa and Henna wrung the water out of their clothes while Velda jumped up and down, shouting curses into the distance. "I hope Odin sends a lightning bolt and sinks your boat! Then I hope a whale eats you!

Then I hope it pukes you back up, then eats you again, then poops you out!"

This went on for quite some time, until eventually Velda ran out of breath (and insults). She slumped down on a rock. "Ugh. What are we going to do?!"

"We have a saying in my land," said Henna calmly, squeezing seawater out of her plaited silver hair. "There is no elk on the ice, until the ice breaks."

Velda shrugged. "What's that supposed to mean?"

"I do not know." Henna wandered off.

Nissa screwed her face up, prodding her temples with her forefingers. "Ooh, I think I remembered something back there… about the Silver Tusk. Yes! It's a special thing, a… a prize sought by many. Legend says it belonged to Thor himself."

"Why does this Ethelfled want it so much?" asked Velda.

"It has magical healing properties, I think…" said Nissa. "She's losing her singing voice."

"HA! You're telling me!" Velda pulled the parchment Freya had given her out from under her helmet. Frayed and yellow at the edges, it showed a cluster of islands: the biggest was horseshoe-shaped, with a gap in the bottom end and a centre island tucked inside. Strange decorative runes marked the sides of the parchment, runes Velda didn't recognise.

"It's a map," she said. "But it doesn't say where to."

Nissa prodded her temples again, but this time she just sucked her teeth. "Nope, sorry, it's gone. I don't remember anything else…"

Henna was standing a little way off, holding a staring contest with a seagull. Her deep, ominous voice carried over the crash of the waves. "They call it, 'The-Completely-Boring-and-Totally-Uninteresting-Map-that-Leads-Nowhere-at-All-and-Absolutely-Does-Not-Lead-to-a-Shiny-Shiny-Prize'. It is known as just 'The Nowhere Map' for short. It was believed lost, but our captain tracked it down. She had to arm-wrestle the famous druid Merlin to get it." She sniffed. "It was no easy task. He smells like turnip, and he cheats."

Velda studied the map again and noticed a tiny drawing of a tusk-shaped object etched on the smaller island. It sat at the top of what looked like a stone tower perched on a huge cliff. Below, a flowing river was sketched in vibrant reds. "Wait…does this map show the way to the Silver Tusk?"

"Yes and no," Henna replied. "It was only the first part of the captain's plan, for the map does not show all the dangers. The waters around those islands are as deadly as a dragon with indigestion." She pointed a bony brown finger at Nissa without looking away from the strangely unblinking seagull. "YOU were the second part of the captain's plan."

"Oh, really? Me?" said Nissa, looking pleased.

"You are a pilot," said Henna. "The best, so they say. Freya spent a long time searching for you, but the day after we found you…" She mimed a huge set of jaws with her hand. "…*CHOMPY-CHOMP!* And now you don't know one end of a longship from the other."

41

"Oh, yes! There was a disagreement over lunch," Nissa said brightly.

"A what?" asked Velda.

"A disagreement. With a polar bear, who wanted its lunch." Nissa pointed to herself and gave a laugh. "That's why I'm so, er…" She drummed her fingers on her chin.

"Forgetful?" supplied Velda. So the story the crew had told her was true.

As if to prove the point, Nissa's eye was caught by a nearby seabird. "Ooh, that bird looks just like my Aunt Gunhild!"

Velda stared down at the map. "Freya gave this to me, and you with it, Nissa. She must want me to find the Silver Tusk. But how, when we don't even have a ship, or a pilot who remembers how to pilot!"

Henna won her staring match, and her feathery

opponent flapped off with an annoyed *"SQUAWK!"*
The woman chuckled and lowered herself onto a
rock, folding her legs and closing her eyes. "Perhaps
we should sit here for a while and think." The others
joined her, until, a moment later, Henna leaned
gently to one side and let loose a long, whining
FART.

"No!" said Velda, holding her nose and jumping to her feet. "I'm not the sitting-down kind."

"Perhaps that's why Freya entrusted the map to you," said Nissa.

"You're right!" Velda punched her fist into her palm. "She said I'd figure it out… She wants me to find the Silver Tusk, I know she does! If I can do that then I can free Freya and the crew! There *must* be a way…"

Right on cue, the plain, square sail of a longship rounded the headland. Velda grinned. "Oi, you two, wave!"

"But what if they want to capture us?" asked Nissa, waving anyway.

Velda straightened her helmet. "Oh, I'm counting on that."

Chapter 7

The longship was crewed by a gang of fierce-looking
Viking men, who growled and waved their swords
as they drew alongside the rocks.

Velda leapt into the boat. "Okay, we give up. You captured us!" she said brightly.

"Er, oh, okay…" their leader said with surprise. "Well, I should think so too!" A short, tubby man with a long brown pointy beard, he angled his sword at Velda uncertainly. "Ahem… Cos I warn you, I am a very, *very* Viking-y Viking!"

"Well, I'm Velda, and I'm even Viking-y-er than you." Velda dodged under his sword and elbowed him in the ribs.

He dropped his weapon. "Ouchy!"

In a flash, she snatched his falling blade out of the air, twirled it round and jabbed it under his nose. "Ha! In fact, I'm the Viking-est Viking of all," she added.

The ship's crew quickly burst into terrified screams, abandoning their weapons. They ran around in chaotic panic, crying, "SPARE US!" One even threw

himself over the side of the ship with a shriek of
"MUMMY!"

Velda's brow creased. This was NOT normal
behaviour for a shipload of ferocious Vikings.

Nissa jumped aboard, snatching up one of the
fallen swords, and leapt to Velda's side, while Henna
drew her bow with a grin.

"P-please, don't!" blubbed their leader, thrusting
his hands in the air. "All is not as it seems!"

On hearing those words, Velda recalled Freya's advice. She withdrew her sword from the man's left nostril. "Whadda you mean?"

"H-He's not really Viking-y," said a tall, thin member of the crew. "He's quite nice, in fact. Lovely table manners, and he sings like an angel!"

"Aw, thanks!" The man blushed. "He's right, though, I am pretty un-Viking-y... We all are. R-Rollo's the name."

"What's with all the growling and the swords, then?" demanded Velda.

Rollo gave an apologetic shrug. "We're just cloth traders. A few days ago, we were on our travels when we bumped into a group of Viking raiders. We didn't want them to beat us up, so we pretended we were just like them, y'know, drinking too much ale and singing rude songs about our enemies' mums.

It seemed to work, but then Wilf here…" He jabbed his thumb at the tall, thin man, who waved his fingers at Velda and grinned. "He won this ship from them in a game of 'Rock, Parchment, Sword'."

"Beginner's luck!" the man added with a shrug.

"Well, we thought it would be fun to try it out for a few days, you know, stealing gold and scaring monks, but we're just no good at it!" said Rollo.

"We're not nearly Viking-y enough," added Wilf. "Plus, I have an ale intolerance." He patted his stomach, then belched loudly. "BURRPP! Oops, pardon me!"

Velda stuck the sword into her belt and propped her fists on her hips. "Well, soz an' all that, but this ship's mine now, boys. I've got an important quest to complete, so you'll have to skedaddle."

Rollo nodded meekly. "Righto, fair enough."

Wilf waved the crewmen ashore. "Come on, lads. Our raiding days are over."

"WE'RE SAVED!" the men cheered, hurrying off the boat.

"Wait," said Nissa. "We're going to need a crew!"

Rollo wailed and waved his hands. "Oh, please, no! Don't take us! We all get terribly seasick – we've only just managed to get rid of the vomit smell!"

Velda wrinkled her nose. "Ew."

"What about that lot?" said Wilf, pointing out some figures huddled at the ship's stern. "We found them, like we found you, marooned on some rocks."

"Who are they?" asked Velda.

Rollo shrugged. "They told us a Viking lord captured them on his raids around Britain, then decided he didn't want them."

Velda opened the pouch Freya had given her and flipped a gold coin into Rollo's hand. "Here. For the ship. That should be enough to get you all home."

Rollo stared down at the shimmering coin. "Oh, you're too kind. Thanks for not killing us horribly and everything!"

"You're welcome," Velda said. "Wait, what's this ship called?"

"The *Mangy Mutt*," Rollo replied, before scrambling away up the rocky beach with a cheery wave.

Velda blew her lips. "That's a rubbish name! I'll have to change it."

"If you change a boat's name you place a curse on it," Henna warned.

Nissa nodded. "She's right there, you know."

"However," added Henna. "You may cancel the curse. By getting a small girl to wee in the ship's bilge."

"Ooh, you're a small girl!" Nissa said to Velda.

Velda glared. "I am NOT weeing in the bottom of my new boat!"

Henna shrugged then thumped her bow on the deck like a staff. "The *Mangy Mutt* it is, then."

Chapter 8

Velda turned towards the figures huddled at the *Mangy Mutt*'s stern. "Oi! Why are you lot so unwanted, then?"

A man eagerly leapt forward. He wore fancy clothes and a long Celtic cape. A tuft of fair hair was swept delicately over his pale forehead. With a flourish, he strummed a small harp, which was badly out of tune.

TWO-INNNGGG!

Then he broke into song in a thin, nasally voice:

*"Unwanted! Unwanted!
We're sick of being taunted!
As insults go, it's really low,
We are NOT unwanted!"*

The tune ended in an excruciating screech and a theatrical bow. "My mane is Nandrake," he announced in an Irish accent.

"Your mane is *what*-drake?" asked Velda.

A girl threw off her tartan shawl and gave a cough. She had fair freckled skin, rosy cheeks and long red hair pulled back in a messy ponytail, and she wore a grubby apron. "Ach! He means his name is Mandrake," she explained.

"Nandrake!" the man declared. "Bing of Kards!"

"He means King of Bards," the girl translated.

"King of Gobbledegook more like," tutted Velda.

"Bing of Kards and Kard of Bings!"

"He gets his words all shoogled aboot," explained the girl. "That's why he sings."

"You call THAT singing?"

Mandrake leapt onto a bench and strummed his harp again, but Velda elbowed him off and he fell on top of the harp with a **TWO-INNNGGG!**

"No offence," said Velda, "but you sing like a constipated whale and my ears have been tortured enough for one day."

She put her hands on her hips. "Anyway… I'm looking for a crew."

The girl with rosy cheeks thrust her hand in the air. "Och, pick me!" In doing so, she accidentally punched Mandrake in the face as he rose from the deck. The musician fell on his harp again.

TWO-INNNGGG!

"Sorry! I'm Bridie," the girl said.

"Sorry?!" grinned Velda. "For punching him, you're definitely in! What else can you do?"

"Well, I'm nae good with an axe, but I can bake. And you've come just in time for some bannocks." Bridie picked up a tray from the ship's brazier, only for it to slip from her grasp. "Ach, I'm always dropping things!"

A hand, rich brown and strong, reached out from under a blanket, snatching the tray at lightning speed and catching the tumbling bannocks before they fell to the deck.

A woman's face peered up from under the blanket. "And I'm always here to catch them," she said, smiling warmly. She triple-somersaulted to her feet without dropping a single bannock, passing the tray to Bridie kindly.

Velda nodded, impressed. "Finally, someone with *real* potential! Are you as speedy with a sword?"

The woman bent down to pick something up from the floor and pulled it over her braided black hair. When she stood up, she was smoothing down the folds of a nun's headdress. "Alas, I am a woman of peace, not poleaxes," she said. "My name is Sister Akuba."

"Odin's beard!" groaned Velda, disappointed. She gazed round at them all – a tuneless bard, an accident-prone baker's girl and a peace-loving nun – and puffed out her cheeks. "Ugh, you're not much of a ferocious Viking crew, but I guess you'll have to do."

Standing up near the prow of the ship, Henna licked her finger and held it in the air. "The wind is coming from the south. Which way are we headed?"

Velda unrolled the parchment, scratching her head as she and Nissa studied it. "How am I supposed to know? I don't know where these islands are. I can't even read the runes."

Mandrake flounced past them and sat sulkily on a bench well away from the group, striking up a mournful tune on his harp.

"Wait!" gasped Nissa, clutching her head. "I just remembered something! These islands on the map, they're called the Islands of Deadly Doom. I think I know the way! If I remember rightly, they're just east of Iceland. It's only a few days' sail…" She reached into her jerkin and yanked out a tiny metal fish dangling on a piece of string. "My compass!" Then she pointed into the distance. "That way, north by north-west!" she said, before rushing to the tiller.

Velda grinned. "Well then," she barked at her new crew, "ready the ship, you stinking pig-dogs, cos we've got a quest to begin!"

Chapter 9

Nissa was like a different person, expertly steering the ship, shouting orders and showing herself to be a first-rate sailor. For a while at least. It wasn't long before her face screwed up and she touched her fingers to her head, slumping into Velda's arms. "Oh, I don't feel so good…"

Velda propped Nissa on a bench, before guiding Henna towards the steering tiller. "Just keep it straight," she said.

"I once crashed a sleigh off a cliff," said Henna, staring into the distance. "That too should have been kept straight."

"I hope you were alright!" Bridie said, while tripping over her own feet and spilling a pitcher of water. "Ach! Sorry!"

"I was," replied Henna with a shrug. "The people it landed on… not so much."

Velda turned to find a withered old man's face far too close to her own.

"Are you the new captain?" he barked, eyeing her closely.

"Where in merry Valhalla did you come from?!" Velda looked him up and down. He had a bushy white moustache and wore nothing but a pair of tight-fitting shorts.

"Well, it's about time for a change of personnel!" the man said in a posh English accent. "Because I have a number of complaints. Firstly, the toilet facilities on this ship are disgraceful—"

Velda rolled up her sleeves. She was about to throw him in the sea, but then Sister Akuba waved from the other end of the longship. "Over here, sir!"

The man turned and smiled. "Ah, waitress, there you are!" He strode towards her. "Can I have my usual table for dinner, please?"

"Who in the name of Thor's stinky socks is he?!" asked Velda.

"Och, that's Mr Egbert," said Bridie. "He's been on this ship longer than we have. I'm not sure why, but he seems to think he's on some kind of holiday."

"I too have complaints," said Henna, who was in the middle of yet another staring contest with a seagull. It was perched on the tiller, its black beady eyes unblinking. "Like, why is this bird always following me?"

"That's not the same bird," replied Velda.

"Hmm," said Henna darkly. "That is what it wants you to think."

For a time, the *Mangy Mutt* coasted the waves with ease. The wind filled the sail, and Velda began to feel good. She was on an epic adventure, she had a ship and a crew (well, kinda) – this was what being a Viking was all about!

But in an instant the wind changed, and so did Velda's mood. A dark bank of cloud swept over them, bringing seas so rough Mandrake looked like he might hurl into his own harp. White-capped waves crashed against the bow, rocking the boat dangerously.

"It's gonnae blow a hoolie!" cried Bridie, pointing at the darkening sky.

"Blow a *whattie*?" Velda asked, following Bridie's finger to see a swirling, thundering, lightning-filled storm heading straight towards them.

Chapter 10

An even-paler-than-usual Mandrake jumped up at Velda's side, trying to keep his balance while strumming his wonky harp.

TWO-INNNGGG!

"A storm! A storm!
It means to do us harm!
I need the loo, what shall we do—"

Velda tugged on a rope, and a beam swung round and whacked the bard on the back of the head. "OW!"

"Get rowing, you yodelling sea rat!" barked Velda, thrusting an oar into his hand.

"But I'm a fartiste! A famous fartiste!" he protested. "I do not woe!"

Velda snatched Mandrake's harp. "I'll chuck this rotten thing in the sea!" she yelled. "NOW GET ROWING!"

Mandrake's lip quivered, then he jumped onto a bench and started rowing at high speed.

As they entered the worst of the storm, they could hardly hear each other shout (or in Mandrake's case, cry) over the roar of the wind and the crash of the sea. They all hunched forward against the driving rain.

Meanwhile, Mr Egbert was sauntering around in his shorts, gazing out at the storm with his hands clasped behind his back. "Ahhh, nothing like a bracing stroll around deck before dinner!"

Velda was about to help him stroll right off the

side of the ship, but was interrupted by a cry of alarm from Nissa.

"Hey! It's a big… big…" She struggled to remember the word, eyes wide. She tapped her bandaged head in frustration.

"Och, I love playing word games on long journeys!" shouted Bridie. "Is it… a bird?"

"A fish?" guessed Sister Akuba.

"WAVE!!" roared Velda, as a ginormous wall of water crashed into the side of the ship. The *Mangy Mutt*'s mast gave a colossal **CRACK!** and Velda looked up to see the heavy wooden beam toppling straight towards her.

Sister Akuba sprang into action. She somersaulted over the rowing benches and cartwheeled across the deck, lifting Velda to safety just as the split mast landed with a **CRASH!**

"Thank Odin for you, Sister!!" Velda cried. "Where did you learn to move like that?"

The nun shrugged. "Before I was a nun, I spent some time in a travelling circus. I was their star acrobat, 'The Amazing Akuba'." She backflipped on the spot and struck a pose, landing gracefully as everyone else on the storm-tossed ship struggled just to stay upright.

Velda gaped at her.

"Don't look so surprised, little one," the nun replied with a grin. "I have lived many lives: storyteller, international singing star – I may even have dabbled in a bit of light forgery for a time, but we don't talk about that." Sister Akuba gave a laugh and fixed her headdress. "Never judge someone by appearance alone – you should know that more than most, my tiny but terrifying friend."

Eventually the storm passed, giving them the chance to inspect the *Mangy Mutt*'s mast properly. The wooden beam was split in two, but still hanging on by a thread, and a huge hole had been ripped in the sail.

"Ach! We're done for!" said Bridie.

"NO!" said Velda. "I *have* to find the Silver Tusk and save my crew."

"I have seen worse," said Henna, squinting up at the broken mast. "Find something tight and stretchy."

"Yoo-hoo! How about these?" cried Mr Egbert, waving his tight-fitting shorts around in the air. Fortunately, he was not naked. He had already changed into his formal eveningwear for dinner.

Velda grabbed the shorts and tested them with a TWANNGGG! "Are these tight and stretchy enough?"

"Hmm." Henna took the shorts in both hands and stretched them as if testing the drawstring on her bow. She nodded, like she was appreciating a good war hammer. "These will do."

"Then let's get this mast up!" barked Velda.

They all formed a line and hauled the split mast back into place using a tow rope, then Sister Akuba shimmied up with Mr Egbert's stretchy pants to bind the beam into position.

"It will hold," grumbled Henna. "But without a sail it is as useful as a salad at a Viking feast."

"We could use this to patch it up," said Nissa, holding up a huge piece of cloth. It was made up of lots of strips of fabric – silk, wool, linen, tartan, even shimmering sequins – and each strip was a different colour. It looked like a rainbow had exploded. "The traders must have left it behind. Ooh, it's so pretty!"

Velda reckoned she was right. Old Rollo and his cloth trader friends must have used it as some kind of sample for customers. All the same, she was appalled. "Ferocious Vikings' sails are NOT PRETTY! You'll be wanting to change our prow head to a unicorn next!"

"But without a sail we'll never get to the Islands of Deadly Doom…" said Nissa.

Velda thought of Freya and the *Valkyrie*'s crew stuck in Ethelfled's rat-infested dungeons and sighed. "UGHH, fine!" she huffed. "Just get this ship moving!"

Chapter 11

That night, the sea was calm. They unfurled the newly patched sail, letting the breeze carry them onwards. Velda had to admit that it didn't look *so* bad. Then again, perhaps it was so ugly it would strike fear into the heart of their enemies.

Bridie doled out bowls of warm porridge and everyone agreed that it was delicious, even Mr Egbert, who was sitting alone at an upturned barrel, a scrap of the old sail tucked in his collar as a napkin.

Their stomachs full, the crew lay around watching the stars. Velda tossed Mandrake back his harp, and he kissed and cradled it like it was a newborn baby. Henna had tuned it, and when he gave it a strum, they realised that the excruciating **TWO-INNNGGG!** had disappeared. It actually sounded good, even with Mandrake plucking it.

"Where did you learn to tune a harp?" Velda asked Henna.

"It is no different from plucking a chicken," replied the old woman, before promptly falling asleep. "ZZZZzzzz…"

As Mandrake strummed, Sister Akuba began to sing, a lilting song of the home she had left long ago to travel the world. The two of them were perfect together, her voice and his harp. Their music rose up into the starlit night.

Mr Egbert applauded. "Bravo! It's about time this ship had a decent entertainment programme!"

Bridie plonked herself down at Velda's side. "Do ye miss your home, Velda?"

"Not really," shrugged Velda. "I miss my friends, Thorfinn and Oswald, but that's it. What about you?"

"Na, me neither," smiled Bridie. "Back home in Pictland, they all told me I was clumsy and daft. I can't help it if my body doesn't listen to what my brain is telling it. The *Mangy Mutt*'s my home now."

Velda stared into the rippling water. "I wonder what Freya's doing."

"Probably in Castle Hengist. That's in Kent," said Nissa. "Oh, wait, how did I know that?" She tapped her forehead with her fingers. "Here it comes again! Yes, it's all coming back!" She pulled out her fish compass before scooting off to adjust course.

Sister Akuba broke off from her singing, letting Mandrake strum on his own. "Did she say Castle Hengist?"

"Yeah, why?" asked Velda.

"I used to be a nun there before Queen Ethelfled banished me. She didn't like my singing."

"HA! That doesn't surprise me – you can *actually* sing! She sounds like a punctured bagpipe!"

Nissa came running back from the tiller. "Quick, Velda, before my memory goes, there's something I have to tell you. And you're NOT going to like it!"

Chapter 12

Nissa unfurled the Nowhere Map on top of a barrel.
They stared down at the Islands of Deadly Doom.
"We know the map was the first part of Freya's plan,
and I was the second, because only an idiot would
sail these waters without a pilot. But part two's not
going so well…" She pointed to her bandaged head.
"Then there's the third and final part of Freya's
plan – the runes." Nissa tapped the strange symbols
clustered around the edge of the map. "Freya was
sure they held the secret to finding the tusk – she
was still searching for a scholar to decipher them
before Ethelfled caught up with us."

Velda could see why the *Valkyrie's* captain had been putting off her quest.

"But you know all that," Nissa rushed on. "The big whopper of a thing I have to tell you is that even with the map, and us somehow figuring out a way to read the runes, *and* me miraculously remembering how to pilot us through the waters, we still might not get our hands on the Silver Tusk..."

"EH?! Why?!" Velda frowned.

"The *wolf*!" Nissa jabbed her finger at the image on the map of a wolf's head.

"Some little wolf isn't going to stop me!" laughed Velda.

"But this is no ordinary wolf. Its name is Fenrir. It guards the only way to the tower where the tusk is kept. It's said it has teeth like daggers and eyes like fire, and that the pass is littered with the bones of all those who've tried to defeat it and failed…"

Velda sighed. "Okay, one problem at a time," she said, trying to think what Freya would do. "We'll deal with the runes and the killer wolf when we get there, but first we need to *actually* get there…"

As Mandrake stopped playing, silence fell, and Nissa touched a hand to her forehead. "Oh, my head, it's jumbling up again."

"Wait!" Velda glanced at Mandrake, then at his harp, then at Nissa, then back at Mandrake. *Hmm, what did all of the times Nissa got her memory back have in common?* She thought back to the crash of the Saxon ships and Queen Ethelfled's shrieking...

Noise! *Could it be noise that brought Nissa's memories back?* Velda yelled over to Mandrake, "Keep playing, you clown!"

The bard looked pleased – for once he was not being asked to shut up. He began to strum, and Nissa jumped up. "Ooh, my memory's coming back again!"

Velda grinned. "Ha! I think I might just have a plan..."

Chapter 13

The following morning, Velda stood at the prow with her spyglass. On the horizon she watched a cluster of islands rise out of a thick layer of fog, the central island topped by a hulking, flat-topped volcano.

The Islands of Deadly Doom.

A thunderous rumble echoed across the sky, and a pall of black smoke belched from the mouth of the volcano. Rivers of red-hot molten lava streamed down its steep slopes.

Velda stepped up onto a barrel. "Right, you layabouts! Now remember, be LOUD! If I see any of you slacking you'll be overboard before you can say 'soggy undercrackers'!"

Wielding pots and spoons and oars and barrels, the crew gathered around Nissa. Even Mr Egbert. "Is this a lifeboat drill? Oh, what fun!"

Mandrake gave a small cough, then began to strum his harp, while the others made noise with their makeshift musical instruments. Henna slammed her bow down onto Mandrake's foot in time, his cries of *"OW! OW! OW!"* creating a pleasant kind of rhythm.

Nissa's eyes flashed bright. "Yes! YES! It works. You were right, Velda. The noise really does bring back my memory!" She rushed to the tiller.

"LOOK!" Bridie pointed her spoon to the right-hand side of the ship, but it flew out of her hand, shot over the side and whacked a passing gannet square in the face.

A giant German galley was approaching, impressively built and manned by a team of powerful oarsmen. It ploughed straight past them, heading towards the islands.

"Ooh, another ship," crooned Mr Egbert, waving. "Hellooo, fellow travellers!"

At the ship's prow stood a tall knight wearing gleaming golden armour. He had a square jaw and a mane of shiny dark hair that fluttered softly in the breeze. He barely gave the *Mangy Mutt* a second glance.

"OOOHHH!" Bridie gasped. "That's Baron Hermann von German! He's the greatest and most famous knight in Europe. One of the girls in the kitchen back home had his portrait pinned up in her quarters. She was forever slobbering all over it."

"EURGH!" Velda gagged.

"He must be after the Silver Tusk too," said Nissa.

"WHAT?!" shouted Velda. "You mean we aren't the only ones?"

"The Silver Tusk is a fabled prize," replied Nissa.

"Many great knights quest for it. Its location isn't a secret. But not all of them have a pilot, and none of them have the Nowhere Map."

Velda caught Baron Hermann's eye. He looked from the *Mangy Mutt*'s mast, held together with Mr Egbert's stretchy pants, to the rainbow-bright patch on the sail and the crew bashing pans like they had all lost their minds, and gave an arrogant smirk. With a flick of his glossy hair, his galley left the *Mangy Mutt* trailing in its wake.

"He's going to get to the tusk before us," growled Velda.

"Oh no he's not," said Nissa. "Just watch."

They stared after the German ship as it cut through the channel between the two islands. It was the straightest and most obvious route into the inner waters, one that Velda would have chosen herself.

But then Baron Hermann's ship gave a juddering
JOLT! Its hull was smashed to smithereens as it
crashed into something unseen below the water.
The galley began to list, and all its crew, including
Baron Hermann, were forced to abandon ship. The
knight flapped around, struggling to keep his head
out of the water, yelling, "My hair! My beautiful
hair!"

"See? No pilot," said Nissa. "They don't call it the Passage of Peril for nothing." She turned the tiller and the *Mangy Mutt* swung away from the channel.

Velda waved at the flailing knight as they skirted past the wreckage. "Be seeing ya, loser! Watch out for sharks!"

With the crew still making as much noise as possible, Nissa piloted the ship along the coast of the outer island. Then she rounded the headland at its tip, leading back down into a narrow channel on the inside.

Velda hung over the prow, watching for dangers and calling them out. Slowly, they glided past deadly rocks and sandbanks, until at last Nissa steered them into the inner waters of the main island and the longship landed with a crunch on the gravelly beach.

High above them, casting a forbidding shadow, loomed the thundering black volcano of Deadly Doom.

Chapter 14

"Okay, now shut that racket up you snivelling weasels!" barked Velda.

The crew put down their pots and spoons and cheered, applauding Nissa's expert piloting.

"Wait!" Mandrake whined. "There's still thwenty-tree verses to go..."

A dazed look came across Nissa's face, and she staggered away from the tiller. "Oh, what are we clapping for?" she asked, joining in.

Sister Akuba nodded towards another galley that was beached nearby. "Looks like we've got competition, little one." A trail of footprints and wagon wheels led to a small encampment on the shore. A few figures milled about, and smoke rose from a campfire.

"Another ship!" Velda rolled up her sleeves and cracked her knuckles. "They better not have beat us to the Silver Tusk!"

"Peace, Velda. Whoever they are, we have something they don't," said Sister Akuba, waving the map.

Velda took it from her, then swung down the rope into the lapping waves and onto the beach, followed by the others. There, she studied the map closely. "But what's the point in having this if I can't read these runes?!"

"Och, why did ye not say? I can read those," came a chirpy voice at her side. It was Bridie, peering over her shoulder.

"You?!" Velda gasped in disbelief.

"Aye. The great lord I worked for back in Pictland was a runes scholar. I used tae sneak into his library and keek at the manuscripts. I taught myself tae read."

"Why in blistering battleaxes didn't you tell me this before?"

"You never asked!" replied Bridie. "Everyone thinks all I'm good for is baking bannocks… and then dropping them."

"So what do they say?" Velda asked.

Bridie scanned her eyes over the symbols. "They're ancient, and very rare." She traced her finger over the first set of runes on the map.

"Beware ye the angered wolf.
To avoid the teeth,
ye must scratch beneath!"

Velda rubbed her chin, thinking of what Nissa had told her about Fenrir, the wolf that guarded the pass, and what Freya had said about scratching beneath the surface. "Sometimes things aren't what they seem…"

Bridie carried on. "The second one says:

"Fear ye the flaming river.
To save your soul,
please bring a mole."

"A mole?" Velda frowned.

"Oops, no sorry…" She wiped a crumb off the map. "A pole, it says *'please bring a pole'*."

Velda's head hurt. "Anything else?"

"There's one more," said Bridie.

"Be ye careful on your climb.
To avert your fate,
don't go straight!"

Velda strode to and fro, trying to work out the clues. Nearby, a figure wearing golden armour hauled itself out of the water. It was Baron Hermann, his long inky hair plastered across his face, knotted with seaweed.

The knight flicked the hair out of his eyes, plucked a crab off his shoulder then stomped off up the beach. Seawater poured out of the joints in his armour.

"Come on, we can't let Baron Square Jaw beat us to that tusk," said Velda, leading her crew up the beach and through a small, gloomy makeshift camp with shabby tents.

Bridie looked at the miserable, hungry faces of the men round the campfire as they twirled a tiny, pathetic piece of barbecued seaweed around on a spit. "Tsk. This place needs a wee bit of brightening up," she muttered, helpfully pinning back the flapping awning of a tent, only to trip over the peg lines. "Och!"

DOINNGG!

All the lines pinged loose. A gust of wind caught the fabric and – **WHOOSH!** – blew the entire tent down the beach, leaving behind it a man snoozing in a camp bed.

"Sorry!" whisper-called Bridie, as the man woke up and shook his fist at her.

They soon came to a low turf rampart with a gateway, where Baron Hermann was combing the sand out of his hair. Three tall bearded men in hooded robes, each bearing a staff, stood blocking the gate.

"We are the Druids of Doom," the man in the middle boomed in a deep voice. As he spoke, a great peal of thunder echoed from the volcano.

"Are they the band for tonight?" cut in Mr Egbert. "Do they take requests?"

"We decide who is worthy to go forth in quest of the Silver Tusk," barked the druid.

"Wotcha, boys! That'll be me then," said Velda,
stepping forward.

"But I am ze most famous knight in Europe,"
crowed Baron Hermann. "I have rescued fourteen
damsels in distress and eleven panicked princesses,
vether zey vanted to be saved or not. Zere is none
more vorzhy zan I—"

His boasting was cut short by a sound so chilling that it silenced the entire camp. Velda shivered, and even the hairs on Henna's chin stood on end.

HAWOOOOOOOOO!

Bridie gasped. "The wolf!"

Chapter 15

Everyone scrambled up the rampart to see a pair of knights come hurtling out of a cleft in the cliff. They'd lost most of their armour and were wearing only their helmets and long johns. One carried a broken lance, the other a bent, blunted sword and mangled shield.

*"**HELP!**"* they wailed, charging down a scree slope and sprinting towards the gateway.

An enormous black shape came bounding out from the rocks behind them. It was the size of an elk, thought Velda, or maybe even bigger. She could see its ferocious teeth and red eyes.

Fenrir.

The two men vaulted the rampart, and then kept going, sprinting off down the beach. Velda watched them go, noticing that the bottoms had been ripped out of their long johns.

"Who were those two clowns?" she asked.

The druids gave her the kind of look someone

would give an insect that had just landed in their soup. "Only two of the greatest knights alive, Sir Percy and Sir Jonty of Malta."

"Huh! Not so jaunty now, are they?" Velda joked, nudging Baron Hermann with her elbow. He was not amused.

"Vhat are *you* doing here?" he sneered.

Velda sighed, rolling up her sleeves. "Stand aside, Baron Pout-a-lot, I'm going to have a go at this wolf."

Baron Hermann glared at her. "How dare you! I vas first in ze queue."

Mr Egbert burst in. "Ooh, is there a queue? What for? Can I join?"

"Baron Hermann is a renowned knight," the druid snapped at Velda. "And *you* are a little girl!"

"Look, mister," said Velda. "I need that Silver Tusk. My captain is relying on me—"

"Don't be ridiculous, *leetle girl!*" Baron Hermann and the druids looked down at her and laughed. Some of the knight's bedraggled men appeared, and they began to snigger too, until they were all bent double in hysterics. "HAHA!" Baron Hermann wheezed. "DO NOT MAKE ME LAUGH! I DO NOT WANT ZE WRINKLES!"

"GRRR!" Velda reached for her axe. "That's it! Pretty boy here's getting his face rearranged!"

Sister Akuba held her back. "Wait, Velda! While I would like nothing more than for you to rearrange this rude man's face, maybe you should use your other strengths this time..."

"EH?! What 'other strengths'?" Velda asked, confused.

"Erm, insulting people?" suggested Bridie.

"Threatening pinnocent meople and their pusical pinstruments?" said Mandrake sulkily.

"Ooh, I know! What about scheming?" said Nissa brightly. "You're good at concocting plans..."

"Hmm... A plan?" said Velda, her brain already working. "To distract this lot away from the ramparts and give me a chance to get through..."

Mandrake suddenly burst loudly into song.

"A plan, a plan,
 oh Velda has a plan,
It feels so great, I cannot wait—"

Velda cuffed him round the head. "SHUDDUP!"
She glanced round the faces of her crew and smiled.
"As it happens, I do have a plan," she said. "Back to
the ship you lot, we've got work to do!"

Chapter 16

Onboard the *Mangy Mutt*, Velda leapt up onto a barrel and yelled, "Alright, listen up! The blokes here are all bored, miserable and hungry, so we're going to exploit that."

"How?" asked Bridie.

"Well, I'm using *my* strengths so it's only fair we make use of all of yours…"

Swiftly, Velda explained her plan and the crew jumped to work, while Nissa went off to 'borrow' some horse-drawn wagons from the camp.

"Oh, is this an activity session?" asked Mr Egbert. "What are we making?"

While the others were busy, Henna helped Velda get ready for the dangerous task ahead.

"You remind me of myself when I was young," the old woman said. "Brave, headstrong, thirsty for the blood of your enemies…"

"Er… thanks," said Velda, picking up her axe and straightening her helmet. "Now let me at 'em, cos I'm SOOOOOO ready!"

In the encampment, the sad faces of the men around the campfire looked up to see a strange sight indeed. A train of wagons was rolling into their midst. A sign hung off the roof of the first wagon, reading: BRIDIE'S BANNOCKS. Bridie held out a delicious-smelling platter, yelling, "Roll up, roll up! Pictish delicacies! Get 'em while they're hot!"

The second wagon's sign read: HENNA'S FORTUNE TELLING. Henna couldn't actually tell fortunes, but they didn't think the men would be excited by a murderous farting granny, so they'd had to improvise a bit. She perched on the back of the wagon, her legs crossed and her eyes closed like some kind of ancient, powerful mystic, though Velda thought she had probably just fallen asleep.

Sister Akuba was performing spectacular feats of acrobatics on the third wagon – flipping and somersaulting and cartwheeling – all while still wearing her nun's habit.

Nissa rolled her wagon in, and music came to the men's ears. Mandrake, standing on top of it, plucked his harp and began to sing.

"A fair, a fair,
oh we have brought a fair!
Let loose your hair and free your cares,
for we have bought a fair!"

Mr Egbert stood on the back, dancing as if there was an eel trapped down his pants.

The men's eyes sparkled and their faces lit up. "A FAIR!"

"FOOD!" a man cried.

"A CARTWHEELING NUN!" exclaimed another.

All the attention in the camp turned away from the ramparts. Men scrambled to eat and dance and be entertained. Even the druids came running to join in.

Baron Hermann went straight for Henna's fortune-telling stall. "Can you zee my future, old hag?" he asked.

"Yes, something is going to cause you great pain," she replied, then clubbed him hard on the head with her bow.

Bridie yelled out at Velda, who had snuck into the camp under Henna's wagon. "Now, Velda! The coast's clear!"

Velda sprinted for the deserted ramparts, vaulting over them with ease.

"HEY, LEETLE GIRL!" screamed Baron Hermann, still rubbing his head. He clenched his fists and stamped his feet. "She is taking my turn! IT. IS. ZNOT. FAIR!"

"COME ON, VELDA!" yelled her crew as they abandoned their wagons and clambered up the ramparts to watch. More and more of the men joined them, some munching on Bridie's bannocks, others nursing bruises from Henna's bow.

Velda snatched up the broken lance, sword and mangled shield that Sir Percy and Sir Not-So-Jaunty had dropped, then crept up the scree slope towards the cleft in the cliff.

It wasn't until she reached the top and gazed down the slope on other side that she spotted it, prowling hungrily.

The wolf.

She'd never seen such a terrifying creature. Its drooling jaws gaped, and its razor-sharp claws glinted in the sun.

Velda thought back to the first clue from the Nowhere Map. "'*Beware ye the angered wolf*', eh?" She steeled herself. "Well, here goes!"

With a mighty roar, Velda launched herself downhill, charging straight for the beast.

Chapter 17

The wolf turned its red eyes towards Velda and raised a gigantic paw, ready to swipe. She dived onto her shield and used it as a sled, ducking down as low as she could. Aided by the scree, she slid right under Fenrir's claws.

"*'To avoid the teeth, ye must scratch beneath!'*" she cried.

Velda lifted her sword but made no effort to thrust or stab. Instead, she jiggled the blunt edge along the wolf's ribs. Tobogganing through Fenrir's hind legs, she scrunched to a halt at the bottom of the slope.

Velda leapt to her feet, ready to run, only to see

the giant wolf rolling around on its back making a strange noise. It took her a moment to realise what it was: a fit of doggy giggling!

The wolf bounded towards her, but now it was friendly rather than ferocious, like an overgrown puppy. Its giant tongue slobbered drool all over her face. "Ha! *'Scratch beneath'* – it worked!" Velda tickled its tummy. "Who's a good doggie?! You are, yes, *you are!*"

She picked up what looked a lot like a human bone and threw it in the air. "Go get it, boy!" The wolf lolloped off after it happily. Wiping the slobber from her face, she turned to find her next obstacle: a stream of molten hot lava running right across her path.

"'*Fear ye the flaming river*'," she said, repeating the words of the second rune. "'*To save your soul, please bring a pole*'."

Velda sprinted for the lava, gripping her broken lance tight. Raising the pole above her head, she plunged it down into the hot stream until she felt a jolt. Then she vaulted, pushing herself high into the air.

"WAHOOO!" Velda arced over the boiling lava and landed with a thud on the other side. "Thanks for the pole, Sir Not-So-Jaunty!"

Ahead, a steep cliff rose up towards a ramshackle stone tower, perched below the dark, smoking summit of the volcano. A light flickered in the top window of the tower. There the Silver Tusk was waiting for her.

Velda straightened her helmet. Two tasks down, one to go…

✳ ✳ ✳

At the bottom of the cliff, Velda could see that it was a straight climb. She could swing her grappling hook and be up the cliff to the tower in no time. Easy.

Except… She thought about the third rune. "'*Be ye careful on your climb. To avert your fate, don't go straight'*."

"Hmm… Don't go straight…" Gazing around, she spotted a mossy ledge which led off to one side, before zigzagging back to the bottom of the tower further up the cliff.

Velda took the narrow ledge, climbing carefully along, bit by bit. Anyone bigger than her would surely fall to a squelchy death below, as proven by the pile of skeletons at the bottom of the cliff. *Ha!* she thought, *sometimes being little is a good thing!*

Along… along… up, then back. Only now did Velda see that there was a crack in the cliff wall just underneath the tower and it seemed to be moving… Peering closer, she could see that it was in fact a nest of poisonous snakes, hissing and spitting furiously. A straight climb would have taken her right past them and to a painful death.

As the volcano rumbled and belched plumes of smoke, Velda climbed the final few feet towards the tower's lit window.

Chapter 18

Inside the tower was a circular stone room, a meagre fire burning in the grate. A wizened old man with a long white beard came hobbling in, squinting at Velda through tiny eyes. "Ah! At last!" he warbled. "I have waited many years to award this prize to a great champion, and here you are!"

Velda was drawn to a shiny object on a stand in the middle of the room. It was beautiful, inlaid with intricate carvings and covered with gleaming metal.

The Silver Tusk.

"I was beginning to think no one would ever succeed!" the old man went on. He heaved the tusk

off its stand, blowing away the dust before dumping the prize into Velda's arms.

"Thanks, Gramps!" Velda beamed. She'd done it. She'd actually found the Silver Tusk! Now all she had to do was get Freya and the crew of the *Valkyrie* back.

"I might finally get a nice holiday now…" the old man rambled. "Somewhere hot."

Velda glanced outside at the molten lava spewing down the hillside. "Okaay…"

The man toddled over to a cluttered desk and flicked through the pages of a large book, then picked up a quill. "For the records, what is your name, good knight?"

"HA! I'm no knight," Velda scoffed.

The old man spat out his teeth. Literally, they flew across the room and out of the open window.

"Wh-what?! Not a knight?! This is an outrage!"
He fiddled furiously with a lens hanging round his
neck, then held it to his eye, looking Velda up and
down. "B-But you're just a little girl!" He reached
out, tugging the tusk back out of Velda's grasp.

"Well this *little girl* just kicked every-knight-ever's
bum. The tusk's mine!" She tugged it back.

"Oh, dear, this is most irregular." He scratched
his forehead with his quill. "I must at least record
a title, I suppose. Every great champion has a title.
What is your name, little girl?"

"Velda," she replied, and he scribbled it down, the
quill tickling his nose.

"ACHOO! Dear, oh dear." He shook his head.
"Just Velda? That's no good – I shall give you a title.
How about... Fair Velda of the Silver Tusk?"

Velda smirked. "Nah! Not my style. How about...

Velda the Awesomest Viking? Anyway, be seeing you, Gramps, I've got a quest to finish. Enjoy your holiday!"

With a cheery wave, Velda the Awesomest Viking climbed back out of the window, the Silver Tusk tucked safely beneath her helmet.

Chapter 19

A few weeks later, the *Mangy Mutt* sailed into Port
Hengist, the capital of Saxon Kent, England. A dark
and forbidding castle towered above the town's busy
harbour.

"Look!" Bridie called out. Velda spied the sleek
shape of a longship tied up at the pier. A longship
with an unmistakeable red-and-white-striped sail.

"The *Valkyrie!*" cried Velda.

"Freya and the crew will be in the dungeons,"
said Sister Akuba, nodding to some barred windows
visible in the rock underneath the castle.

"Now we just need to get inside." Velda noticed

two tough-looking guards with ugly bowl-cut hairdos at the end of the pier. "How do we get past the bad-haircut brothers over there?"

She thought about it as they tied the boat up and made their way up the pier. A diversion? Or just fight their way in? She licked her lips – the last option was the tastiest. She reached for her axe…

Suddenly, the two bowl-bonced guards fell to their knees. "Lord Egbert!" they gasped. "Everyone thought you were dead!"

"Oh, goodness gracious, no," chortled Mr Egbert, stepping forward. "I've just been on my holibobs. I do love a nice cruise."

He turned to Velda. "A huge thanks to you and your crew, Captain. Yes, a thoroughly enjoyable trip. Especially your jester." He nodded at Mandrake.

Mandrake staggered about like he'd just been assailed by a volley of rotten fruit. "Ex-SQUEEZE me! I am SSSNOT a jester! I am a FARTISTE! A great FARTISTE!"

Mr Egbert gave them a jolly wave. "Enjoy your shore leave, you've earned it! Do feel free to pop into the castle for a goblet of mead."

The guards watched Mr Egbert, or rather *Lord* Egbert, toddle off up to the castle, then glared back at Velda and her crew.

"You heard the man!" said Velda, pushing past them.

"Well that was easy! We got in without causing a scene," said Bridie, before colliding with a stack of lobster pots, which toppled to the ground with a colossal **CRASH!** "Ach, sorry!"

"Stop apologising, Bridie. And remember the plan, you lot!" said Velda, as they passed through the castle gates.

"The flan?" Mandrake burst loudly into song.

"A plan! A plan!
Oh Velda has a plan—"

Velda jabbed her elbow in his ribs. "Will you shuddup about flans and plans!"

Nissa touched her forehead. "A flan? Hmm... No, I don't remember anything about a flan..."

"Don't worry, little one," said Sister Akuba. The nun turned open the seam of her robe to reveal a set of metalworking tools tucked inside and gave Velda a wink. It turned out that blacksmithing was yet another job Akuba did before she became a nun. "We'll head for the dungeons. Queen Ethelfled is in the throne room, up there." She pointed out a round tower with stained-glass windows. "She'll be giving her daily concert right now. She makes everyone sit through it, whether they want to or not."

"I'll listen out for the sound of someone murdering a cat, then," said Velda, nodding farewell to her crew before slipping into the shadows.

Chapter 20

In the top tower of Castle Hengist, Velda followed the sound of high-pitched screeching to a large throne room, where yawning courtiers sat around a stage. A man wearing a pained expression was playing a lute and, to one side, a sad-faced old glazier was getting down off a ladder, having just finished replacing some windowpanes.

Ethelfled flounced across the stage, wearing her shiny armoured breastplate. Long hair waterfalled from under her crown, trailing behind her like a hairy veil.

Velda swaggered right up to the front and

dropped the Silver Tusk at the queen's feet. "Oi, Your Royal Screechiness! There's your tusk!"

Ethelfled's singing shrieked to a halt as she eyed the shiny prize. The courtiers gasped (probably with relief).

The queen bent down, but lost her balance and tripped over her long hair, faceplanting on the stage with a **CRASH!**

The sound of her heavy metal breastplate echoed like a bell, **PRANNGGGG!** Then it pinged off to catapult across the room, narrowly avoiding taking a courtier's head off.

Still, the queen only had eyes for her prize. Grabbing it greedily, Ethelfled held the tusk aloft. Her eyes glinted, and she grinned a horrible black-toothed grin. "At last! The Silver Tusk is mine. Now my voice shall be forever young!" She gave a theatrical laugh, "HAHAHEHOOWAHAHA!"

"Forever young?" said Velda. "Pff. I've never heard worse singing in my life, and I'm a Viking. We invented bad singing."

Ethelfred glared up at Velda. "*You* obtained this?"

"Yup," said Velda, hooking her thumbs in her belt. "So I'll be having my captain and my crew back now."

Ethelfled gave a shrill "UP!" and two guards rushed forward. "WATCH THE ROYAL HAIR!" she screeched as they tiptoed over it to heave her back to her feet. Once upright she gave Velda a smug, superior sneer. "HA! Let that bunch of stinking Viking thieves out of jail? I don't think so!"

"I thought you'd say that," replied Velda.

Ethelfled gave a cruel laugh. "Oh, did you? And what are you going to do about it, *little girl*?"

Velda smiled. "You know, some people – and things – aren't always what they seem. You should remember that. Oh, and give these poor people here a day off from your shrieking."

Ethelfled stared round at her courtiers' faces, horrified, before a man at the back piped up. "Hear, hear!"

"Anyway, must dash." Velda raced to the window and swung it open. Outside, the sun shimmered across the harbour as the familiar prow of the *Valkyrie* cut through the water. Its crew were all aboard, waving up at the window as they sailed off, their celebratory belches echoing on the wind.

Trembling with rage, Ethelfled opened her mouth and gave a high-pitched *"NOOOOOOO!"* Every window in the tower shattered, showering everyone with glass. The poor glazier, who'd just packed up, gave a weary sigh and unfolded his ladders again.

Ethelfled growled at Velda. "You little RUNT!" Her guards approached and Velda windmilled her axe, beckoning them with a grin before whacking them both in the stomach. She leapt onto the windowsill.

"But that's a sheer droooppp!" Ethelfled called operatically.

"Oh, I know," said Velda, securing her grappling hook and rope. "See ya!" And she jumped out of the window, speeding down the tower to the sound of Queen Ethelfled's furious shrieks.

Chapter 21

A little while later, the *Valkyrie* and the *Mangy Mutt* were moored side by side in a deserted bay, far away from Ethelfled's clutches.

Freya stood on board the *Valkyrie* with her hands on her hips, laughing heartily (she had really missed doing that). "Well done, Velda!"

"OORAH!" chorused the crew.

Velda jumped aboard, then pulled something from under her helmet. Something long, thin and sparkly.

The Silver Tusk.

She dropped it into Freya's hands. "There you go, Boss."

Freya frowned. "But I thought you gave it to Ethelfled?"

"Nah!" replied Velda. "Not the real one, anyway."

"But how?"

"Easy really. We paid a visit to the Island of Certain Death's souvenir stall on our journey back. You know, a cheap drinking horn can pass as a pretty convincing fabled prize, especially if you've got someone with forgery skills as good as Sister Akuba's!"

"Ha!" said Freya. "Ethelfled didn't spot the difference between the real tusk and the fake?"

"Nah, sometimes things aren't what they seem, right?" Velda grinned. "You taught me that."

Freya laughed. "Well, the seas are waiting and full of adventure. We must be off! I've heard there's a big reward being offered for a missing German knight."

"OORAH!" yelled Velda.

"Not you, Velda."

"Wh-What?"

Freya nodded towards the *Mangy Mutt*. Velda's friends were looking over at her expectantly. Mandrake with his harp, Nissa with her bandaged head, Bridie with a tray of freshly baked bannocks and Sister Akuba in her nun's garb. All apart from Henna, who was off having another staring match with a seagull. Actually, now Velda thought, that *was* the same bird.

Another head poked up from behind the ship's side. It was Lord Egbert, who was lying on deck sunbathing, holding a curved piece of armour underneath his chin to catch the light. It looked suspiciously like Queen Ethelfled's breastplate. "Helloo!"

"What are you doing here?!" asked Velda.

"I signed up for another cruise, of course," called Lord Egbert. "I enjoyed the last one so much, I decided to do it again."

"But… But…" Velda stared out to sea, then at the *Mangy Mutt*, then finally at Freya. "Joining your crew, that was my big chance—"

"I know, I know, to be a real Viking. Ha!" Freya's bellowing laugh rang out. "Listen to yourself. You've been on a great quest, captured a ship, commanded your own crew, sailed through storms and sprung your comrades from a dungeon. You *are* a real Viking. You're the Viking-est Viking there is!"

Velda sniffed then shrugged. "I prefer 'awesomest'…"

Freya pressed the tusk back into Velda's hands. "Here, this is yours. You've earned it."

Velda was too stunned to reply. Freya lifted her up in a giant bear hug, then dangled her back aboard the *Mangy Mutt*. "I'll miss you, Velda."

Velda nodded. "I'll miss you too, Boss."

"What will you do now?" Freya called as the two ships parted, one heading north, the other south.

Velda smiled. "Oh, I think we're ready for a new quest." She leapt up onto a barrel and growled at her crew. "What do you say, you snivelling pig-dogs?"

"OORAH, Captain Velda!" they cried. "OORAH!"

LONGSHIP NAME GENERATOR

Like Velda and the *Mangy Mutt*, every good Viking needs a longship name that will make any enemies wet their pants. Follow these simple steps to find out yours...

1. On what *day* of the month were you born? Use this to find the *first* part of your longship's name.

1. Burping
2. Whiffy
3. Grotty
4. Scabby
5. Ratty
6. Grumpy
7. Whining
8. Smelly
9. Soggy
10. Moaning

11. Pooping
12. Stinky
13. Shabby
14. Sulky
15. Belching
16. Rotting
17. Farting
18. Crabby
19. Puking
20. Mouldy

21. Pongy
22. Crusty
23. Whingeing
24. Manky
25. Reeking
26. Musty
27. Slimy
28. Grouchy
29. Scruffy
30. Grimy
31. Moody

2. In which *month* were you born? Use that to find the *second* part of your longship's name.

January: Dragon   **July:** Hawk

February: Warrior   **August:** Vulture

March: Raider   **September:** Serpent

April: Wolf   **October:** Kraken

May: Marauder   **November:** Demon

June: Falcon   **December:** Invader

For Example

David MacPhail's birthday is **22nd May*** so his longship's name is:

The Crusty Marauder

What would your longship's name be? What about your friends' and family members' ship names?

*Please send any cards, pressies, massive cakes etc. to 76 Hackenbush, Indgar Village, Norway.

Richard the Picture-Conqueror

David the Story-Chief

David MacPhail left home at eighteen to travel the world and have adventures. After working as a chicken wrangler, a ghost-tour guide and a waiter on a tropical island, he now has the sensible job of writing about yetis and Vikings. At home in Perthshire, Scotland, he exists on a diet of cream buns and zombie movies.

Richard Morgan was born and raised by goblins on the Yorkshire moors. After running away to New Zealand to play with yachts and paint backgrounds for Disney TV he returned to the UK to write and illustrate children's books. He now lives in Cambridge, England, and has a family of goblins of his own.